Mary Lyn Ray

ILLUSTRATED BY
Lauren Stringer

Red Rubber Boot Day

Voyager Books • Harcourt, Inc.

Orlando   Austin   New York   San Diego   Toronto   London

Special thanks to my mother, Marla Stanford Stringer,
for playing with my kids in the sandbox,
in the leaves, in the snow, and in the puddles
so I could paint this book.
—L. S.

www.HarcourtBooks.com

First Voyager Books edition 2005
Voyager Books is a trademark of Harcourt, Inc., registered in the
United States of America and/or other jurisdictions.

The Library of Congress has cataloged the hardcover edition as follows:
Ray, Mary Lyn.
Red rubber boot day/by Mary Lyn Ray; illustrated by Lauren Stringer.
p. cm.
Summary: A child describes all the things there are to do on a rainy day.
[1. Rain and rainfall—Fiction.] I. Stringer, Lauren, ill. II. Title.
PZ7.R210154Re 2000
[E]—dc21   97-25676
ISBN 0-15-213756-4
ISBN 0-15-205398-0 pb

TWP 5 7 8 6
4500227959

The illustrations in this book were painted in
Lascaux acrylics on Arches 140 lb. watercolor paper.
The display type was set in Minister.
The text type was set in Goudy Catalogue.
Color separations by United Graphic Pte. Ltd., Singapore
Printed and bound by Tien Wah Press, Singapore
Production supervision by Pascha Gerlinger
Designed by Lydia D'moch and Lauren Stringer

For Allyn,
born in the month of rain
—M. L. R.

For Cooper,
who loves to read books inside
and puddle-jump outside
—L. S.

I press my nose against the screen
and smell the smell of screen and rain.

I listen. I watch.

I may decide to get my crayons
and draw the things I like to draw.

Or I may build block cities.

I may read.
I like to read when it rains.

I may play cars.

Or cave.
My best cave
is my closet.

If it's a slippery, window-splashy rain,
I make a party with my dishes.

And if the rain is raining still,
I go outside. I run.

I am leaf. I am fish.
I swim by Mr. Humphrey
who lives next door,
standing in his yard
with no shoes on.

And Mr. Humphrey says to me,
"It is a fine thing
feeling wet grass
on bare feet
in green rain."

I think splashing in boots is better.

Red boots. My boots.
Red rubber made-for-rain boots.

I like slapping, stirring puddles.
I like a day for boots.

But when I wade into blue sky—

I'm glad the sun is back!